Kimberly F. DeMeo

One Little Egg

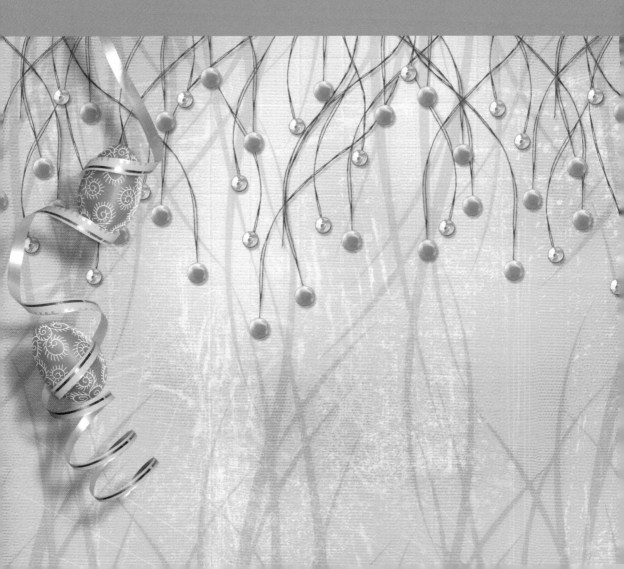

One Little Egg
All Rights Reserved.
Copyright © 2013 Kimberly F. DeMeo
v3.0

Illustrated by Julia Andrzejewska
Illustrations © 2013 Outskirts Press, Inc. All rights reserved - used with permission.

Outskirts Press, Inc.
http://www.outskirtspress.com

ISBN: 978-1-4787-1084-4

Outskirts Press and the "OP" logo are trademarks belonging to Outskirts Press, Inc.

PRINTED IN THE UNITED STATES OF AMERICA

outskirtspress
DENVER, COLORADO

For Jason who has given me the world and
my girls who came along to complete it.

This Book Belongs to:

_____

"Rise and shine recruits!" a voice roared over the speakers. "It's time to go to class."

Exsie is the head egg in charge at the Donor Egg Academy. It is her job to explain egg donation to all of the new eggs who arrive each month. Exsie loves her job, and is always so excited to share her love of egg donation with all of the new eggs, or "recruits" as they like to call them.

The new group just came in last night, introduced themselves to Exsie and each other, and then went straight to bed. She would be meeting with this group any minute.

"Miss Exsie! Miss Exsie!" a young egg screamed. "My roommate Sara won't get out of bed. She seems very sad and refuses to come to class! What should I do?"

Every once in a while this happens; a new egg gets upset that she has to leave her biological woman, and it makes her feel confused and unwanted. Exsie knows that it is her job to show these eggs that they weren't just given away because they were undesirable. On the contrary, they are very special and have a very important job to do.

Exsie turned to the egg and said, "Don't worry about a thing; I'll take care of Sara. Go on to class and I will catch up with you all later."

Exsie then phoned another administrator to see about having her classes covered for the day. "I think I am going to have to do some one on one instruction with one of the new recruits. Thanks. I will see you tonight." She locked up her office and headed over to Sara's dormitory.

Exsie gently knocked on Sara's door. She peeked inside and saw her in bed.

"Go away!" Sara yelled. "I don't want any visitors." She slid all the way under the covers and Exsie heard her mumble, "It's not like anyone wants me around anyway."

Exsie felt badly for her. She had gone through this transition herself a long time ago, and understood what Sara was feeling. "Come on sweetie," she gently said, "talk to me for a second. What do you mean no one wants you around? Don't you know that you are here to learn about a very crucial task that you are needed for?"

"You must've made a mistake. I'm the loser who was given away by my biological woman. She didn't want or need me, so no one will ever want or need me. I'm useless." She sunk her head deeper under the covers.

"Okay, okay………. let's go for a walk. You'll feel better after getting some fresh air. Come on!" Exsie forced the covers back and pulled Sara out of bed.

"Ugh. Where are we going?" Sara asked.

"You'll see when we get there." Reluctantly, Sara walked out with Exsie.

While walking through the campus Sara noticed how happy and confident all of the more mature eggs looked. "I won't fit in here at all," she muttered. She thought to herself that no one would want to be friends with an egg who was just given away for no reason.

"Don't be so sure," Exsie stated with a wink to one of the other administrators.

Sara became slightly curious as they walked out of the campus and got onto a bus, but she didn't want to show her curiosity to Exsie.

After about a half an hour, the bus arrived at a corner of a beautiful little neighborhood. Sara followed Exsie off of the bus and they walked, in silence, for about ten minutes. Finally they came upon a quaint white house with blue shutters and a white picket fence. Sara imagined that there must be a very happy family living inside, and life for them is probably perfect.

"Come on," Exsie whispered as she walked up to a window in the back of the house, "and don't let anyone see you."

Sara climbed on top of Exsie and peaked inside of the window. At the kitchen table sat a very pretty woman with blonde hair and hazel eyes. She had a very kind face, but it was completely filled with sadness. All of the sudden a handsome man walked up behind her and put his hands on her shoulders; he then gently kissed the top of her head.

"Don't worry honey," she heard him say to the woman, "maybe it will happen next month." Then the woman started to cry. Sara felt such heartbreak while watching this couple.

"What's the matter with them? How can they be so sad when they live in such a perfect house? Did one of their kids do something wrong?" Sara asked Exsie with an inquisitive look on her face.

"That's the problem, Sara," she responded.

"What's the problem?"

"They don't have any kids. Come on, let's take a walk and I will explain." Sara jumped off of her shoulders and walked along with Exsie.

"So why don't they have children? Don't they want them? Don't they like kids?" Sara started to think about how she, herself, was given away, and thought that maybe these people didn't like children. Just like her biological woman didn't like her either.

"Ok, ok. Let me answer one question at a time. First, let me start by saying it's not that they don't want children, it's that they can't have children. They actually want a baby more than anything in the world, and have been trying to have one for many years," Exsie began.

"So why don't they just have one?" Sara asked. She didn't understand what the big deal was. "Men and women get married and have babies all the time."

"Well, it's not that easy for everyone. Let me tell you their story and then maybe you will understand." The two continued to walk through the quaint little neighborhood.

"See, when Ken and Jeanie met they fell very much in love. So they got married, bought the perfect little house, and decorated all of the extra bedrooms in anticipation of filling the rooms up with lots of children. But with each passing year there was still no baby. They would hope, pray and wish upon stars, but still nothing! So Jeanie went to see the doctor and received very bad news. She did not have something inside of her that is essential in order to have a baby."

"What? What?" Sara questioned. She was so interested in their story that she forgot all about feeling sorry for herself.

"You see Sara, every woman needs to produce eggs inside of her in order to make a baby."

"Eggs? Like the ones you eat?" Sara asked.

"Not eggs that you eat, a different kind of egg. Unfortunately, Jeanie couldn't make eggs inside of her. Because of that, Jeanie and Ken were very sad. They thought that there was no hope for having children, and that the rest of their lives would be very unfulfilled and lonely."

Sara really felt terrible for them. "Too bad that there is nothing anyone could do to help them."

"Well," Exsie began, "as a matter of fact, there is! Come on, let's head back to the Academy and I will explain. It's getting late and something very important happens there each night at 8:00 p.m. I don't want you to miss that."

The two hopped on the bus back to the Academy where Exsie continued explaining everything to Sara. "So you mentioned having someone help Jeanie and Ken. Well, as it turns out, they have decided to ask someone to help them fulfill their dream of having a baby."

"Who did they ask?" Sara questioned curiously.

"They asked our Donor Egg Academy for help. Jeanie and Ken Medeo came to us a few months ago and told us that they were unable to have a baby because Jeanie does not produce eggs inside of her. Our Academy can give Jeanie an egg to use so that she can have a baby!"

"Wait a minute?! Where exactly do these eggs come from? Do you mean an egg like me?"

"Exactly like you, Sara. You were not sent to the Academy because your biological woman did not like you and just wanted to get rid of you! Your woman decided to do something extremely giving so that she can help people, just like Jeanie and Ken, who cannot have children on their own."

"Your biological woman is able to make a lot of eggs, and when she is ready, she will be able to have as many children as she wants. In the meantime, because she makes an abundance of eggs, she decided to donate one to the Donor Egg Academy so it could be given to a couple just like Jeanie and Ken Medeo."

Sara thought about this for a minute and then asked, "So what happens to the egg when it arrives at the Academy?"

"The doctors at the Academy will mix the donor egg with an important part from the man, and then the mixture will be placed inside of the woman's belly. If all goes well, the woman will become pregnant and in nine months the couple will have a baby of their very own!" Exsie concluded.

Sara thought long and hard before responding. "So my biological woman didn't dislike me? She donated me because she wanted to help a couple in need? That makes her a very kind and compassionate person; not at all what I first thought about her." As they pulled up to the bus stop near the Academy, Sara continued to think about how she was loved after all.

Exsie and Sara then hopped off the bus and walked toward the Academy. "So you see Sara, you are a donor egg and that makes you very special! You should be very proud because someday you will help a couple achieve their dream of having a baby."

As they approached the Academy, Sara noticed every egg running toward the center of the courtyard and wondered what was going on. Exsie explained that each evening at 8:00 p.m. an announcement was made as to who would be the next lucky donor egg to go to a family in need. This is a great honor, and every egg there was hoping that her name would be called.

"Come on Exsie! I don't want to miss this!" Sara yelled while running toward the center of the courtyard.

One of the administrators from the Academy walked up to the podium. A hush came over the crowd as she began to speak.

"I am about to announce the name of the next donor egg who will be given to a man and a woman who need help starting a family. We are so proud of this young egg. She will be donated to Jeanie and Ken Medeo, and will help to make all of their dreams come true! And ....that donor egg is............ Sara!"

The crowd erupted with applause and congratulations for Sara.

Sara cried tears of joy and ran over to hug Exsie. She was so proud and so excited that she was going to be able to help Jeanie and Ken Medeo. She loved them already, and couldn't wait to become a part of what she knew would be the most loving and happy family ever.

CPSIA information can be obtained at www.ICGtesting.com
Printed in the USA
BVIW12n0019251017
498056BV00003B/9